ALBERT'S STORY

PART 1

RONALD DEAN DURBIN

ISBN: 978-1-63950-303-2 (sc)
ISBN: 978-1-63950-304-9 (e)

Writers Apex

Gateway Towards Success

8063 MADISON AVE #1252
Indianapolis, IN 46227
+13176596889
www.writersapex.com

CONTENTS

BOOK I

THE ACCIDENT

Chapter 1

DECEMBER 14, 2030

This is the story of Albert Mendoza surviving a horrific crash on Minnesota's State Highway 77 and the young steward Allie, who saved his life. Allie and her elder brother Chandler were raised by their grandmother in Al's Trailer Park in a small suburb in San Antonio. A neighbor, Ron Blain, had been keeping a close eye on the kids. He put them into some nice school clothes and helped keep food on their table. Grandma's trailer was falling apart. Ron's trailer was fourteen years old but in great shape. Ron had just moved into a really nice place on four acres, so his trailer was empty, and Grandma asked if she and the kids could move in there.

Allie and Chandler's parents were a couple but not married. The parents seemed to be interested in many things, but the kids were a low priority. So they were living at Grandma's, and she was feeding, bathing, and taking care of the kids daily. Mom was both near and far.

She and her elder daughter, Sue, also had been raised by Grandma and helped move everything over to Ron's trailer. That night, they had partied with some meth. The next morning, one of the guys who had stayed the night in the trailer threw his cigarette into the yard. Seven hours later, it had turned into a grass fire, heading to Ron's trailer.

The fourteen-year-old wooden front porch burned quickly, getting hot enough to catch the trailer on fire. Sue was in the back of the trailer with her little daughter when she went to see what all the noise was. Flames were now into the kitchen and living room. Sue and her little daughter made it out the back door safely.

The local police and firefighters would get there, but the house was a total loss. Terry, the kids' mom, had been at the doctor's office with Grandma. Ron was also called, and he came. Allie and Chandler, seven and eight respectively, were still in school but would arrive soon. The police chief asked Ron point blank, who had slept in the house the night before, "That would have been Sue and her daughter and Terry and her other daughter, Allie." To make a long story short, meth was found, Terry was tested for it, and her drug test on-site was positive. She was then cuffed and taken into custody. Testing positive for drug use was a violation of her parole. The kids now belonged to Grandma's care totally.

Ron and Grandma had another parent meet the school bus before it got to the burned-out home. Then they went to the home where the kids were and broke the news that everything they had was now gone—clothes, toys, furniture, etc. That afternoon was spent replacing things that one just had to have. Grandma was on oxygen and needed a new machine. The kids had no clothes at all. The Red Cross came through in a big way. They showed up at the fire scene and set into motion getting those necessary items replaced. Grandma was given some cash to get the kids new clothes.

There was now the question of where the kids would spend the night. Ron was still unpacking boxes at his new place but invited the family to stay with him for two months. After that, they would look at the situation and see where they were.

The parents of Allie and Chandler were brought into court and read the riot act. They were told to complete a dozen different tasks, including rehab, or face losing custody of their kids. For the time being, the court placed the kids officially in the home of Mr. Ron as the kids called him. He and Grandma became foster parents to the two. The kids' mom, Terry, would complete rehab in jail but would not finish the total list of tasks given to her by the court. Dad never came back to court after that first visit.

After one year, the court was set to meet. On a Friday before the court date, the child protective staff, the kids, the lawyers, Terry, Ron, and Grandma all met. It was clear that Terry was not going to get the kids back right at this time. The judge would give Terry an extension or remove them forever. As the meeting started to break up, Ron said, "Just a minute, please. The possibilities for care of the children will be decided next Friday." At this point, the kids were whisked out of the meeting. "I don't think Terry is going to keep custody of the kids. If Grandma is given custody, that's okay, but she moves out of my house and into her own. Otherwise, I want full custody of the children." Without much discussion, it seemed that Ron would get single custody of the kids unless the judge gave Terry an extension to complete her tasks.

Ron, looking into Terry's eyes, said, "I don't want to raise your kids. I would just be keeping them for you until you are ready to be their mom 24/7." Ron was far from perfect. He just saw two lost kids who needed a home. If the court removed them, then he would see if the court would let him keep them.

That next week in court, the judge said there would be no extension. Custody of the kids would go to the state of Texas. Terry then asked the court if the neighbor Mr. Ron could adopt the children. Later, after their biological father did not appeal the ruling, Ron Blain—at the age of sixty—became the official guardian of Allie and Chandler.

Actually, nothing changed. They stayed in Mr. Ron's home during and after the adoption process. The kids moved into Mr. Ron's home and stayed there through high school. In school in their small suburb of San Antonio, they were always known as the Blains. Ron was simply their stepdad. That explanation worked for both Ron and Terry.

Allie was into sports and the other things young ladies liked to do. She could have been but was not the valedictorian. After high school, she fled academia. Only after working for five years and not making much money did she decide to go back to school. She didn't have a passion for it, but she was getting certified as a school counselor. At the time of the accident, she only needed her student teaching to get certified. There might be more schooling down the road, but she was about to achieve her first goal.

Losing custody of her two youngest children was like a defibrillator reaching to Terry's soul. She was devastated. At first, she stayed away from the kids. Then Grandma brought them to see her. From that day forward, she worked her way back into their lives. Her two elder children saw her change and encouraged her. Little by little, she worked her way back into being a full-time mom for Allie and Chandler.

In today's world, if Allie had any real problems, it was that she was way too smart for the average Joe. Also, some ladies need to work at being pretty. Allie woke up being the most gorgeous redhead in San Antonio. For now, she was working at the Twin Cities of Minneapolis–Saint Paul International Airport as a steward. It was paying her bills.

In case you were wondering about Chandler, he graduated from Texas State University in five years with a master's in mechanical engineering. He immediately began working in his elder brother's company.

Chapter 2

Albert Mendoza was a first-generation United States citizen while being a second-generation mason. His father, Alberto, stopped in San Antonio's south side. He made a good living working as a mason. Albert was the firstborn of three. Jennifer and Jessica Marie would keep San Antonio as their home. During Albert's teen years, in his free time, he worked side by side with his father and made some nice change. After high school, he got certified as a junior mason through the local south side junior college Palo Alto.

That was where his classroom education stopped. As a junior mason, he was earning some great money. When Alberto was asked by a Minnesotan company who his best mason was, he could truthfully answer it was Albert. Albert's life changed from that of a South Texan to a Minnesotan. Albert accepted a position in Baseline Brick of Saint Paul.

While several guys were vying for leadership positions, Albert simply made award-winning buildings. Soon he was the go-to guy. Also, he took whatever job the company wanted him to do. As a result, he was now the highest paid mason in the company.

Albert was not all work and no fun. He met and married Liz. They had three teens, who can spend as much money as he can bring in. On the night of the accident, Albert was trying to get to Denver to put in a bid on the exterior of the new Denver City Hospital. He wouldn't make it.

Chapter 3

Allie had trouble keeping a guy friend. As soon as they discovered just how smart she was, they would move or become not available or some such thing. Her current was Bob. "Hey, honey, be sure to take your heavy coat. There's some Canadian air headed this way."

Already, the temperature was below zero. For late December, that was pretty cold. "I'm wearing it, but thanks."

Karen was a new steward with the airlines that Allie had trained. "Okay, guys, let me get out of your way. Allie, see ya in a few days. Bye, Bob."

Allie almost followed her out the door. The cold was partially blocked by her super coat, but it was just flat-out cold. Parking at the airport was not a problem, and her shuttle took her to her security area. Flight crews had basically no security checks. They were just waved through.

Allie arrived as her coworkers were boarding their Boeing 787. She liked Drake, the pilot. His copilot was a jerk. Allie was the number two steward after Rhonda. Rose, Dave, and Ann filled out the crew. Rhonda had everyone doing their preflight checks. With all things in order, she notified the captain, "We are ready to board, Captain."

"Roger that."

Allie's position for boarding was the first exit row. She could help people get settled without being in the way. Albert met Allie in this exit row. He had seat 26A. Allie gave her best smile and greeting as Albert stored his briefcase and coat and then took his seat. Albert didn't lay many bricks anymore, but he was still tanned because he was Hispanic. His sweater was of the V-neck variety, and he wore a nice dress shirt with khaki slacks.

Allie's job was to make the passengers feel comfortable and forget they were traveling on a piece of metal. "Hi, I'm Allie. Is this your first trip to Denver?" ·

Albert was going to Denver, but he would not let this girl tell him where he was going. "I could be going to Dallas."

She had taken in his not-quite-casual wear, the briefcase, and his strong hands. Her hand went to her forehead like a mind reader might do. It was like Johnny Carson. "Let's see. You are going to Denver. You have a meeting with some Suits guys, but you won't try to impress them because they already know how good you are. Your buildings have won some awards for your company. Your construction company is sending only you because they know you are enough. You have laid a lot of bricks. So now you are talking to people about how much money and time it will take for your award-winning company to take the job. Does that sound pretty close?"

"Okay, I'm going to Denver. By the way, I'm—"

Allie held up her hand to stop him. Her hand went to the forehead again. "You are Albert Mendoza."

Besides being gorgeous, this lady seemed pretty smart. "Okay, how'd you do that?"

Allie had her fun, so she confessed, "I saw it on your briefcase." So she had cheated, but that didn't explain the rest of it. "All the other stuff?"

While they were visiting, Allie was finding just the right place to stuff carry-ons, directing traffic, and doing other steward jobs. "You're in construction and, I'm guessing, a mason. Your hands are strong, and your face says you are outside a lot. Your attire is casual but not sloppy. You put your briefcase away, so you are not a rookie. You are alone, so you must be good at what you do. Award-winning buildings? Just a hunch. You look like you have it together."

This was the most amazing person he had met this week. "Do you have a family, Allie?"

"If you mean a husband, no. I've got two brothers and a sister. They all live in Houston."

Allie didn't normally talk with one person as much as she was with Albert. "And you?"

"My wife and kids live here. I'm gone a lot. I hate to say I live here. I visit here. Really, I'm from San Antonio. And before that, my father came from Mexico. He got a green card and turned it into a U.S. citizenship."

Allie now felt free to share a little personal information that she never shared with passengers. "My boyfriend and I share an apartment here. But I'm really from San Antonio also."

Albert shared his philosophy on working away from home. "Never go home unannounced. Always call. You don't want to find any surprises there. I always keep my wife informed of my schedule."

"You're kidding? You are as much saying it's okay for her to have other guy friends."

"I'm okay with her having company. I just don't want to know about it. I'm gone a lot."

The captain came over the intercom. "Welcome aboard flight 153 to Denver and then onto Dallas. It's gotten really cold outside, so we have to deice before we take off. It will add another fifteen minutes to our takeoff time. Sorry about that. Cabin attendants, please be seated." With that, flight 153 taxied over to the deicing area.

What might have been the coldest air ever was blowing down off the ice in northern Canada. The winds were topping eighty miles an hour. Outside at the moment, the temperature was at a negative forty and still dropping. Before the plane was deiced, the captain came back on the intercom. "Sorry, folks, but we are not going anywhere. The Denver Airport has cancelled all flights in or out and is shutting down."

Albert's face showed anger and frustration. "Allie, I need to get to Denver by tomorrow. Bids need to be turned in by the sixteenth."

"Surely a couple of days won't hurt?"

"I've got to try. I'll just have to drive. My Jeep has four-wheel drive." Albert had made a friend. He decided that he needed to warn her one more time. As they parted company, Albert told Allie, "Call before you go home."

"Be safe, Albert." Both smiling, Allie reached for her phone and then decided not to call.

Her car barely started. Her heavy coat was penetrated by the cold. She would be glad to get home and out of the cold.

As Allie pulled into the gated complex, she noticed Karen's car. It wasn't in front of her place, but it was her car. Curious, she hurried into her place quietly. There in her bedroom were Karen and Bob. "I guess I should have called before coming home."

Allie picked up a book and threw it at the bed. That felt pretty good, so she found another unbreakable item and threw it. As she threw things, she was screaming, "My two friends fucking on my bed in my apartment! Karen, get out! You too, Bob!" Allie had been betrayed by her fiancé and her good friend—two betrayals. "Karen, get out now!"

Bob had not intended to break up with Allie. He just wanted to have a lot of sex with whomever. "What, I live here!"

"Not anymore, you don't! This is my place. Get out! Get out! I'll be back in thirty minutes. Also, leave the keys." Then Allie stormed out of the apartment. Her head was spinning. One more disgusting romance was over. Her tears were freezing on her face. The car was still warm, and she was grateful. She soon found herself on State Highway 77, heading south. She knew she needed to get back home and out of this weather.

Just minutes ahead of her, Albert turned south on State Highway 77. Albert knew he could pick up I-35 and keep going south. He was hoping to get ahead of the crazy storm. The wind was really blowing and rocking his Jeep. He looked down for a moment and backed up just in time to see the cars in front of him spinning and crashing. He slowed down and pulled over. However, he was now facing the oncoming traffic. In that moment, the car behind him went airborne. There wasn't time to do anything.

Suddenly, the Jeep had its top ripped off, giving off a giant explosion of energy. A piece of glass sliced through Albert's face. One moment, he saw it happening; and the next moment, he was dead, except his body didn't know it because it froze as did the top of his skull. Albert lay dead on the cold, frozen earth. His skull was another twenty feet away with the top of the Jeep.

People were walking around, checking on everything. Jere punched in 911. "Several cars found some black ice. We have one fatality. We'll need several ambulances." He continued giving more details. There on the ground was a jacket, and he covered the dead body.

In front of Allie, traffic slowed, and then she was soon inching along. Allie needed to find a place to turn around and go home. As the turnaround came closer, she noticed a green Jeep off to the side of the road. Six cars had collided, and the Jeep seemed to have gotten the worst of it. The whole top was missing. There were no police cars there yet. Everyone seemed to be okay, but she didn't see Albert. If that was his Jeep, where was he?

On a crazy impulse, she pulled over to see if Albert was there. People were walking around, checking on one another. There on the ground lay Albert, covered with a jacket. Why was he covered with a jacket?

Slowly, she walked toward the covered body. Behind her, she heard a voice saying, "Lady, leave the jacket alone. He doesn't have a head." Allie raced to the jacket and lifted it. It was Albert. Too much had taken place in the last few minutes. This can't have happened to Albert. Now in shock, she walked slowly toward the top of his Jeep.

Going at over 60 mph, cars started flying through the air. One flew over Albert's. The window came out of the door and sliced through his skull. His bottom jaw was intact. Everything above it was sliced off. The spinal cord is a bundle of nervous tissue. The medulla oblongata connects it to the brain. At the foramen magnum, the spinal cord was cut and frozen all at the same time. No spinal fluid was lost, just frozen. There was no unfrozen blood. The outside temperature hovered around minus-fifty degrees. Cryogenics was functioning naturally. Albert was frozen.

BOOK II

ALBERT'S RECOVERY

Chapter 4

The top of the Jeep was about twenty feet away. Moving like a zombie, Allie made her way to it. Next to it was his skull. She slowly bent and picked it up. The teeth were all gone, but otherwise, it seemed to be in good shape. It too was frozen.

Her slow movements caught the eye of Anne Craft, a resident physician at the local VA hospital. She was in training, but she recognized shock. "What are you going to do with that?"

There was a person now blocking her path. Unstable and about to faint, she got out, "I'm going to give it back to Albert. He lost it." Allie tried to step around the reason she couldn't go forward.

Anne reached for the skull, but Allie refused to let her have it. "I need to give it back to him." Allie was shaking her head no.

In a firm but soft voice, she said, "My name is Anne, and I'm a doctor. I can help you." Allie was standing upright, but nobody was home. Her body was on autopilot. She did release his skull. Anne didn't think it would hurt the dead man, so she and Allie walked over to Albert's body, and Anne replaced the skull exactly where it needed to go. There was a clicking sound, like LEGOs snapping together. "How's that?"

"You're the doctor. But it looks like that's where it belongs." Allie was in shock and crying. She sat down next to Albert. Maybe "collapsed" was a better word.

With hurricane force winds and temperatures around a negative fifty, it was not good for any living thing to be outdoors. Now there were flashing lights as those people who covered an accident began showing up. Sirens were sounding, and traffic was being rerouted. An EMT guy looked at Anne and Albert. Anne shook her head. The EMT guy, Josh, covered Albert with a blanket. Allie moved to sit on part of his blanket. The ground was very cold. Then she took his hand. He was frozen like his skull.

Dr. Anne didn't like Allie still being outside in the cold. "You need to come with me and get out of the cold."

"I'm not going to leave Albert alone. I'm going to stay with him. I'm Allie Blain, a steward from his flight. It was cancelled, so Albert was going to drive to Denver." Allie was still in shock, but she was going to sit right there next to Albert.

Josh placed another blanket around Allie. She looked up and smiled. The strong winds made any movement difficult. Allie knew she couldn't stay there long, but did that really matter now?

Anne went off to help other people, leaving Allie and Albert alone. After about fifteen minutes, the shock began to wear off. Allie started talking to Albert. "What a crazy world we live in. I'm not sure I want to live in it any longer. When I went home tonight, I caught my boyfriend in bed with my best friend. How could they do that? I caught them fucking on my bed. They were fucking me. I know you told me to call, but I don't want a relationship like that."

Albert woke up feeling nothing and seeing nothing. He kind of went down a checklist. But nothing was working. He couldn't move any part of his body. He could hear Allie talking. He tried speaking, but nothing happened.

"My sister Sue's had a rough life, but she made some bad decisions and paid for them. Her two kids are doing fine. Eric raised them. Eric and Chandler are doing great. Eric's been married for a while, and Chandler got married a few years ago. Albert, what's wrong with me?" Allie cried, her tears freezing.

After crying softly for about ten minutes, she started talking with Albert again. "I know you're dead. So whatever I say to you will not be repeated. I'm going to stay with you until they put you in the vehicle to carry you to the morgue. Then I'm going home for the last time and take twenty sleeping pills. I just want to end it." Allie continued crying, not for Albert but for her own messed-up life.

Albert remembered flying through the air, and then everything went black. He couldn't see or feel anything. Everything was still black, but he could hear Allie talking. He tried moving, but nothing worked. He couldn't move his head or open his eyes. His legs and feet didn't respond either. Then he heard Allie say he was dead and that they were going to take him to the morgue. He screamed; his middle finger moved. No sound came out, but he moved his finger.

That little movement caused Allie to scream and jump up. "Oh my god! Oh my god!" She jumped up and was now looking down at Albert.

Things had settled down quite a bit. The injured were being sent off to Anne's VA hospital. So Anne came over to see why Allie was up and about. "What's going on, Allie?"

"He's alive. He just twitched."

Albert had no idea where he was and what was happening, but he knew he was alive.

"Allie, I assure you Albert is dead. Dead bodies sometimes twitch."

Albert seemed to be like in a black box, separated from everyone and everything. He wanted to communicate with them to let someone know that he was alive. His body was not responding to his commands.

For a moment, Allie had forgotten how depressed she was. Now it all came back down on her, and she was swirling down in an even deeper depression. Crying, she muttered, "Albert, stop moving. You're dead. Soon I'll join you."

Albert knew he was still alive. He was surrounded by blackness. It was almost as if he were in a coffin. With that thought, he screamed no. But there was no sound. He did feel his middle finger move again.

Allie reacted as if a 110-volt electric shock just passed through her. There were no words, just a scream. Anne had not gotten very far away and looked back at her. "Did he do it again?"

"He's alive. I swear he's alive."

Albert, in his blackness, was agreeing with Allie. *Yes, I'm alive.*

"Allie, people don't live after losing their skull."

Albert again was thinking, *Oh, that's not good.*

"Next, you're going to say you are just upset. You are absolutely right. I am upset on several different fronts. When I told Albert I was going home to take an overdose of sleeping pills, he twitched the first time. Right now, I told him he was dead and that I would be joining him soon. He twitched again." Allie was crying again.

"Allie, honey, he needs to do it for me. Okay?" Anne was trying to act as if she believed Allie.

Albert's only contact with the outside world was his middle finger and Allie. He tried to move it one more time, but nothing happened. Anne placed her hand on the bottom, and Allie put her hand on top. "Albert, I need you to twitch the middle finger again. Anne's hand is on the bottom. She wants you to signal her that you are alive." Nothing happened.

Now Allie was crying again. "Albert, I know you're hearing me. You can't give up. If you give up, then I do too. If you die tonight, so will I. Are you going to let me die?" At the end, her words came in sobs and screams.

Albert could hear his new friend Allie, but nothing worked. Then he screamed at God, *Are you going to let her die?* Still there was no sound, but he twitched.

Through her tears, Allie said, "Thank you, Albert."

Anne also thanked him. Shaking her head, she couldn't believe what had just happened. "Josh, get over here. We need one more ambulance."

Inside his box, Albert was smiling. He could move his finger.

Anne pulled the blanket off Albert. Allie was surprised. "What are you doing? He's alive."

"And I'm trying to keep him that way. Have you heard of cryogenics? He's alive because he's frozen. We need to keep him that way. He's going to need a pacemaker because his heart is not beating. He's going to need oxygen because his lungs are not working. We can take care of that at the hospital but not here. We need him frozen until we get to the hospital."

Josh brought the ambulance over to where Anne and Albert were. Albert was put in a neck brace and loaded into the ambulance. Anne and Allie both got in for the ride to the hospital.

The frozen Albert arrived at the VA hospital ER. The head ER doc was Mark Spence. "We're not the morgue. Why are you bringing me a dead corpse? Get him out of here."

Anne knew logic would not work with Mark. He was a by-the-book kind of guy. "Mark, you will be the first doctor to treat a decapitated patient who survived. I can see the headlines now: 'ER doctor Mark Spence successfully treated the first ever person to lose his head and survive.' You won't be able to live a normal life after this."

Mark liked how all that sounded, but it couldn't be true. "What are you smoking? I give you the day off, and you buy some pot?"

"The top of his head was separated from his spinal cord, but he's able to work his middle finger. He's alive. We need to ventilate him and get his heart working. We can continue this conversation after we've done that."

Mark let Anne go and do her thing. But this other civilian needed to get out of the ER. "Would someone escort this lady out of here?"

Anne had started setting up what needed to happen to Albert, but she had to break away and explain to Mark why Allie needed to stay close. "No, Mark. He communicates with her. We need Allie to stay close."

Mark had about had it with this crazy young doctor. "Okay, we are back to what you are smoking."

Anne thought, *Okay, plan A didn't work. I need to go to plan B. I need to make an offer he can't refuse.* "You don't have to believe anything I've said. Just give me a couple of hours with these two, and you will become famous. If I'm wrong, then I'll quit, and you'll be rid of me."

All of the above sounded good to him. Anne was a royal pain in the ass most of the time. She cared too much about her patients' welfare. That would kill a doctor. "Okay, Anne, you've got two hours, and get this girl into some scrubs."

Albert was fully thawed. The cardiologists took longer than Anne had thought it would to attach a pacemaker. All was finished now. "Your time is up, Doctor. Either he moves his finger or we shut everything down and move him to the morgue like we should have."

Albert, in his black box, was hearing everything and could almost see. His lids were closed, but he was sensing light. He hadn't heard Allie since he woke back up.

Anne called for Allie. "Okay, he's been given a pacemaker. We have him breathing. Now we need him to move for us, or they will shut all this equipment down."

Albert had thawed. His body was working, but he couldn't feel anything. Everything was still dark. The sensor was tiny, and he couldn't feel it. Anne was talking, but he hadn't heard Allie's voice.

"Hello, Albert. This is Allie again."

Albert, inside his black box, was smiling again, happy to be in touch with Allie.

She placed her hand on top of his so she didn't touch the sensor. "I'm going to need for you to move your finger again." The whole ER staff was watching this crazy lady talk to a corpse.

Inside his dark closet, Albert tried to move his finger and then anything. Then he tried screaming. He wanted to communicate with Allie. He didn't care about anyone else. During the last several hours, some film or something had moved in to block his impulses. The cervical nerves connect the fingers to the brain, but somewhere in between, some film was not letting the electrical pulses pass.

After watching Allie try a few times to get Albert to communicate with the outside world, Mark said, "Okay, we've wasted enough time and money. Pull everything off the corpse."

Inside his black box, Albert was screaming at Allie, but nothing was happening. Nothing was moving. Albert was going to die.

The breathing tube was now removed. Allie went crazy, screaming, "No! Albert! It can't end this way!"

Mark grabbed Allie and tried to pull her away from Albert, but she wouldn't move. Now she started pounding on Albert's chest, still screaming. Mark was able to pull her away with some help.

Inside his black box, Albert was screaming. Again, he was shouting at God.

Allie got in one more final blow. "No! Albert, twitch!" And he did. The sensor beeped. The whole room became quiet.

Mark was stunned, and he dropped Allie. The impossible had just happened. The sensor beeped again. Whatever had been blocking the neuron pathway moved when Allie started beating on Albert's chest. Now all the ER staff were clapping.

Allie now screamed again, "Albert! You did it!" She was jumping around, screaming, and clapping.

Anne started undoing what Mark had put in motion. "Get that breathing tube back in."

Albert was excited. He could hear all the commotion, and he liked it. The sensor went off one more time. There was more clapping as the director of neurology walked in. She too couldn't believe what she saw take place. Cheryl Hastings moved into the ER clapping. Mark couldn't believe what had just taken place. He was silent, but Cheryl wasn't. "What the hell is going on here?" Cheryl was number two at the hospital.

Anne spoke for the group. She told Dr. Hastings what had just transpired. Dr. Hastings was incredulous. She had been waiting twenty-plus years for a miracle like this, and Dr. Spence was trying his best to kill the survivor. "Mark, you are lucky I don't fire your ass on the spot. We don't fight against people trying to save lives. We work with people trying to save a life. Anne called me right now. You should have called me when this first happened. Mark, go home."

"I can't go home. My shift isn't over. What had happened here tonight couldn't have happened. This is all madness."

"Your shift is over for tonight. Pray that you're not fired after this." Like the general she was, she gave several orders, and they were all followed without question. "Nurse, let's get this patient to neurology ICU. Anne and Allie, come with me. We have some things to discuss."

Chapter 5

Cheryl had access to millions. There were federal and private monies for research into spinal cord regeneration. When word got out that someone had been decapitated and survived, more money would flow in. Mrs. Mendoza would need to release Albert to the hospital for research. Anne could get moved to neurology and then did Allie want to continue being involved with Albert's case.

Cheryl's mind was spinning. What should she do first? "Anne, bring Allie to my office right now."

Being number two at the hospital had some advantages. Cheryl had a nice office with a conference room attached. She was in charge of neurology, but much more as assistant to the director of the hospital. The three met in the conference room. "Let's begin with you, Anne. Do you want to be assigned to neurology? That would mean you would no longer be a resident."

"Yes, of course. But there's so much I don't know."

"You started this. You believed in Allie and Albert. There's no better person than you to work with Albert. We have a staff that can answer your questions or point you in the right direction. But you cared enough about Albert to bring him here instead of the morgue."

Anne just nodded okay. She was just about to become a normal doctor with normal hours. The green stigma would pass away. Her smile was as big as it had ever been.

Then Cheryl gave her attention to Allie. "Young lady, this is a fine mess you've gotten us into."

Allie recognized that famous line. "Laurel and Hardy?"

"You don't know what you've done, but you have just changed the world forever. Until tonight, no one had survived losing their skull. You did this by replacing his. Now the next step is for you to come and work for us," Cheryl said. Allie was just shaking her head no. "Again, you don't know what I'm asking you to do. I'm not asking anything of you except to be the go-between, working with us and Albert."

Allie had a job already and knew nothing about neurology. She would stay a steward. "I'm a steward. I work for an airline."

Cheryl knew that all this was a big surprise for Allie. She would need to ease up to the job offer. "Is that your final goal in life?"

"I'm a semester away from being certified as a high school counselor."

"Is that your final goal in life?"

"It was a step, a job. It was going to pay me $60,000 annually. I don't know what my final goal in life is. I just know I want to make a nice income."

"Okay, I can offer you $100,000 for this first year and let you go do the last semester of college."

Allie didn't seem surprised with the offer, nodding. "I can live with that." Allie thought about her car being left at the scene of the accident. "Is it possible to get my car towed to the hospital parking lot? It's still at the accident site."

Anne jumped in, "Cheryl, let me take care of that. My car's there also."

Just nodding, Cheryl went on to say, "I'm going to need to communicate with the Mendoza family." By now, Cheryl had been handed a biography of Albert Mendoza. "We should tell the family the truth. Albert is alive but just in a vegetative state. They can come and see him. I recommend that they do not touch him or talk with him." It would make letting him go that much more difficult.

"We can give the wife, Elizabeth, one million and a divorce decree. She then will be free to live on." Cheryl didn't know if she could do it, but she would try. "Just so you know, none of the money I've been spending tonight is coming out of this VA hospital's budget. The veterans will keep all their benefits. This money will begin coming out of a fund for spinal cord injury research."

Mrs. Mendoza thought Albert might be calling to check in; the phone number was local but not his. "Hello."

"This is Dr. Cheryl Hastings at the VA hospital just north of the airport. Am I speaking with Elizabeth Mendoza?"

"Yes. Is something wrong?"

"Yes. I'm sorry to bother you at this late hour, but Albert's been involved in a terrible accident. We have him here. He's in a coma right now. Your first instinct would be to come on over and see him, but with the weather like it is, I recommend coming over tomorrow. He's resting. Again, he's in NICU in the VA hospital just north of the airport."

"Okay, I'll be over first thing in the morning. Thank you for calling."

Liz gathered her three kids and broke the news about Dad. All were upset and not sure what the morrow would bring.

Anne's and Allie's autos had been towed to a nearby garage and would get picked up in the morning. Because of the frigid weather, both spent the night at the hospital. In the basement, there were staff quarters for those on call and other things that might pop up.

They both showered and put on medical scrubs. The machine provided a Coke, sandwich, and chips. The end of the most amazing day in Allie's life ended quickly. She was asleep as soon as her head hit the pillow.

Chapter 6

DECEMBER 15, 2030

By morning, Dr. Hastings had divided up the neurological intensive care unit (NICU) into quarters. Albert had his own quarter with only one way in and out. No one would be allowed to see Albert unless Dr. Hastings approved. Albert would not hear any unwanted chatter. No reporters would be allowed near him. He did not need to hear what other staffers might say. Anne, Allie, and other staff members had free access to Albert, but all others would need permission from Dr. Hastings. Anne could order any medical procedures, and those people could come and go as needed.

While Allie continued to rest, Anne was up and at work in the NICU. She was getting a small office just outside Albert's chamber. Albert was placed in a medical coma to allow his body to recover from the shock of the previous day and to let his body start healing. He had a pacemaker to regulate his heart and a breathing tube to give him oxygen.

Liz arrived at 0800 hours at the NICU. "Hello. I'm here to see my husband, Albert Mendoza. I believe Dr. Hastings is in charge of his care." "Yes. Hello, I'm Cathy Johnston, one of the NICU nurses. Dr. Craft is in charge of your husband. Dr. Hastings is in charge of neurology. Let me take you to your husband and Dr. Craft."

"Thank you."

The nursing station was in the center of the NICU and just steps away. Again, Albert was in a room with one door in and out. Anne was in the outer chamber sitting at her desk when Liz, Mrs. Mendoza, appeared. Liz was five three with dark hair. She was in great shape for her midforties.

Cathy entered the office part of Anne's work area. "Dr. Craft, this is Mrs. Mendoza. Mrs. Mendoza, Dr. Craft." Then Cathy excused herself.

Anne told the short version of last night's events. "Good morning. As you can see, Albert is resting quietly. He is in a coma. Last night, several autos crashed, with Albert's getting the worst of it. I came upon the accident right after it happened. Albert's Jeep had its top cut off, and so did Albert. Last night, Albert had his skull separate from his body. This was enough to kill him, but his body froze, cryogenics."

Anne waited a moment for that to sink in. "A steward from the same plane that Albert had been on passed by the accident. Albert had told the steward he had to get to Denver and would just drive his Jeep. The steward, Allie, saw several vehicles that had crashed. One of those was a Jeep. On an impulse, she pulled over to see if, in fact, it was Albert's Jeep. Allie had just had a big fight with her boyfriend. Then she found Albert dead. It was too much for her to consider. She was in a state of shock. She found Albert, and then she found the top portion of his skull.

"Last night when we were out there, it was at least minus fifty degrees. Albert froze instantly. His skull did the same. I saw Allie walking with the skull, bringing it back to Albert. I took the skull from Allie and placed it back where it needed to go.

"I figured Albert was gone. It wouldn't matter whether I replaced it or not. Albert was now given a blanket, really to cover up a body. Allie refused to leave him. We covered her with a blanket as well. The short version of the story is we brought Albert here and put him on life support. He responded. Soon we will run a series of tests to see what got reconnected. You heard me say his spinal cord got separated from his brain. No one has ever lived before after having their spinal cord severed. Frankly, Albert should be dead. Again, for all of us, this is a first."

On the other side of the glass lay Albert. His body looked like Frankenstein's monster. His hair had been shaved. The skull had several staples holding it to the lower portion of his head. Tubes were running in and out of him.

Liz had a chill run through her body. This was her husband. He had been a good husband. The family had everything they needed. Now what would they do? Liz hadn't cried to this point, but now she started. How grief works is strange. Missing Albert's income came to the forefront. Liz would miss Albert, but now how would she and the kids survive?

Anne continued on, "The truth is we don't know if Albert will live through the day. If he recovers at all, we doubt he will ever work again. Mrs. Mendoza, this is all uncharted territory."

Anne wasn't helping Liz feel more comfortable. Now her fears exploded. "No, this can't be happening. I've got three teens to support and a mortgage to pay," she said, almost whispering through her tears.

Anne knew what Cheryl had been thinking, but it needed to come from her. "Let's call Dr. Hastings down here. She's going to want to speak with you."

"Dr. Hastings, I have Mrs. Mendoza here."

"Anne, bring her to my office." It was a short walk to Dr. Hastings's office. They would meet in the attached conference room.

Introductions happened, and coffee was served. Dr Hastings began, "Mrs. Mendoza, this will be hard for you to hear, but a miracle occurred last night. Your husband lost his skull. The steward from the cancelled flight retrieved it and brought it back to him. The temperature was around a minus fifty. Your husband froze, and so did his skull. Dr. Craft happened onto the situation. In an effort to not upset the steward, Dr. Craft replaced the missing skull exactly where it needed to go. Still in a state of shock, the steward stayed with your husband. Blankets were now brought, and Albert thawed a little bit. When the steward told Albert she was considering ending her life, Albert twitched. This is not uncommon for a corpse. But he did it again and then one more time for Dr. Craft to witness.

"Albert was brought to our hospital as a patient. After taking care of things like a pacemaker and a breathing tube, we asked Albert if he was still with us. The answer is that he is alive, with only the slightest of connections to his brain. His hearing is fine, but his only way to communicate with us is his middle finger.

"Albert is in a bad way. Here, we want him to survive. You have a family to take care of. You can't collect any life insurance because Albert is still hanging on to life by a thread.

"We at the VA would like you to sign over Albert to us. If you are willing to release Albert to us, we will be responsible for all his medical costs, and we will give you one million from our research funds for you to take care of your family. I also recommend you let our attorneys give you a divorce decree. We will pay for all legal fees. Also, we'll leave his insurance in your name. Of course, you'll have to tell us who you have your insurance with."

"A divorce?"

"When we talk about Albert getting better, we are talking about taking baby steps. Albert probably will never work again. He probably will never walk again. Right now, his brain is alive and functioning. He can move his middle finger, and his hearing seems to be okay. We have induced a medical coma so his body can heal. All those little things that got cut need time to fuse back together.

"Recovery could take years, if ever. I recommend you and the kids try to move on. If he ever speaks again and some of those other things like moves his body parts/limbs, we could update you. You understand no one has ever lived before after having cut their spinal cord."

Everything was overwhelming Liz. "I would say go forward with your plans. When you get your stuff ready, then I'll give you my final answer." She knew the final answer had to be yes, but she would talk with her teens first.

"I can agree to that. Again, we are sorry about the accident but looking forward to seeing what Albert can do in the future."

"We can't do a DNR because you've already given him a pacemaker. Be reasonable with him. He would want his organs donated if he should not survive."

Hands were shaken and goodbyes said. Liz made one more trip by Albert's new home. Again, the scene reminded her of *Frankenstein*. Albert's head had been shaved. Where his skull had separated, there were a hundred staples. Other tubes ran here and there. He looked dead. His face was swollen. His chest had several staples in it as well. She knew this would be the last time she would ever see her husband alive. And she sobbed. Now she needed to talk with her kids.

The schools in the area were closed because of the winter storm. Liz told her children, "Your father's head separated from his body. He shouldn't be alive, but your dad is holding on by a thread. The hospital wants us to release him to them, and they will do everything in their power to help him recover. The hospital will pay all his medical bills. Also, they know we need Albert's income to keep this home. They will also pay us one million."

Mike and James were numbed by the news and just sat there. Jessica got up, ran to her bed, and bawled. Liz gave her a few moments alone and then went into her room. Liz didn't speak. She just rubbed her daughter's back. No words were going to bring back her father. So she rubbed her back just to let Jessica know that she was there.

Jessica finally spoke. "Can we see him?"

"You can, honey, but he's not the dad you remember. I would like you to remember him from yesterday. He was happy and laughing."

"Okay, Mom."

Mark knew that Dr. Hastings had wanted to keep the name of the decapitated person anonymous, but he couldn't tell his story unless he released Albert's name. In Mark's version of the story to the reporter, Mark was the hero, going against the VA's management. He alone saved the life of Albert Mendoza. The TV stations picked it right up as the newspaper had already gone out. Even the national news was at the hospital by noon. It was a public relations nightmare. Mark laughed. He knew his job was secure now.

When Mark went in for his evening shift, he was confronted by several reporters. He quickly fought his way through, only to find Dr. Hastings there to, in fact, fire him. She knew he had been the source of the leak of the name. Mark was no longer the hero who saved Albert's life. He was an unemployed ER doctor.

Dr. Hastings set up a briefing to share what they knew and how Albert was doing. Mrs. Mendoza was confronted at her home, but she kept saying she had no comment. Her teens were stunned by all the commotion. She asked her teens to not make any comments.

The media did not give up easily. However, after a week of pestering, they quietly went away. Mark hadn't released Allie's name, so she was free to come and go. Drs. Hastings and Craft were met at the door each time they came and left.

After three days, Albert was mending well, so Anne began her inspection. Albert had several checks with those letters like MRI and CT. When they were all done, Anne simply went around his body with a small hammer, tapping everything. One buzz was yes, and two was no. After Allie's pounding, Anne found that Albert could also move his ring finger. He could hear and see, but his eyelids were not working. Albert still needed the equipment to breathe for him. He had tubes to feed him and give him antibiotics. His body was digesting the food and passing it along.

Medical techs took care of his body's needs. Allie did some physical therapy with Albert and stayed in the room with him as long as she was awake. His body was still too sensitive or frail to move out of the NICU. The hospital moved Allie's belongings to an apartment right next to the hospital. She wouldn't have to go to her bedroom anymore and remember what had shaken her so badly that frigid night.

Anne went into the equipment available in the pool for spinal cord injuries. There, she found a pair of goggles that could raise and lower the eyelid by using a magnet. A little metal strip was placed like mascara above the lashes. Then the magnet could raise and lower the lid. It had adjustable settings like a windshield wiper. The goggles would also dispense a small amount of tear. Again, this amount was adjustable. This was all possible with a Bluetooth connection.

Dell donated a special tablet, and Bill Gates and Microsoft donated special software for Albert to control his equipment. The index finger punched the keys while the ring finger moved the cursor. The tablet worked like some smartphone software; it would suggest your next word.

Albert had two fingers working. He could see and use his tablet. But he had no control over the movement of his head. Anne's people developed a way for him to turn his head left and right and up and down. All this was done through the tablet and Bluetooth. Albert had plenty of time to learn how to operate his new equipment. He wasn't going anywhere.

Chapter 7

As the first few weeks passed, Albert learned how to operate his new equipment. With his two fingers, he could type on his tablet, work his eyelids, and turn his head left, right, up, and down. Of course, he had no voice, so communication was a problem. The engineers connected a voice to his tablet, so it became his. Still, it was one tap for yes and two taps for no. The medical techs did their job like clockwork. He was hooked up to several machines measuring this and that. They all were important and had to work together.

Allie had started back to school to finish the student-teaching part of her degree. After her work at school, she would come and do some physical therapy with Albert. His emotions were always higher when she was around. She talked with him like he was a normal person. Many others spoke to him as if he couldn't hear all that they were saying. He chose not to listen to much of what they said.

Albert asked for and got a few channels on his tablet. He wanted the world news. He selected the movie channels, mostly watching the older movies. He had followed the sports teams from Minnesota. For football, he liked the Vikings; but when they weren't playing, he'd watch Green Bay.

With his tablet, he was able to turn the lights on and off. He could ask for things by using his voice box. Life was much improved from when he was lying on the ground after his accident.

When she finished her schoolwork, Allie and Albert would watch a movie, and then she would leave. She hated going to her empty apartment, and Albert hated for her to leave. His body had healed from the wounds of the accident, and soon it would be time to start the experiments, so life had to stay the same.

Chapter 8

SEPTEMBER 15, 2031

After five months, Allie graduated with her BS in education with a major in counseling. Ron Blain, the man who adopted her, was gone. Grandma and Grandpa had passed as well. But her mom, all her Texas siblings, and in-laws and their kids came to her graduation. It was great being reminded that she was not alone in the world. She promised a visit to Texas soon. Then they all left.

She was also grateful for her free time. Now into September, she was ready for something to happen, but it wasn't.

Time passed, but life stayed the same for Albert. Liz and the kids never came to see him. They went on with their lives. Liz got her money and a divorce from Albert.

Albert missed Liz, but he knew she would find company. He missed his sons, but he knew they would carry on. What bothered him the most was not having Jessica around. She was born in December and was a Christmas gift to Liz. But from day one, Jessica was a daddy's girl.

Right after her birth, Albert held his little girl. Her brown eyes burned into his soul. Anytime he was on the sofa, she was there next to him. As a toddler, he'd have to help her get up. She couldn't speak yet, so no words were exchanged, but she was where she needed to be.

At four, she was sitting on his side reading, coloring, watching TV, or just taking a nap. It was the place she needed to be. As she got older, he seemed to be gone a lot. But whenever he was home, she was with him. So he was worried the most about Jessica.

Every two months, Anne and her staff would try a different formula experiment on Albert with no change in electrical impulse connections. Nothing had changed so far. Albert was ready to quit, to die. He spoke to Dr. Hastings about those feelings.

BOOK III

THE MIRACLE

Chapter 9

OCTOBER 15, 2031

It was time for some changes. Dr. Hastings called Allie into her office. "I understand you have your BS now?"

Allie sensed there was more to the question. "That doesn't really sound like the question you wanted to ask."

With a wink and a smile, Cheryl said, "You're right. What's next for Allie?"

"I'm not sure, but that's not the question you wanted to ask me."

Still smiling, the doctor said, "No. I wanted to ask you if you were interested in becoming a doctor."

"So that's the question? No, I don't want to leave Albert. I'm his only real friend. And things aren't going so well with what they've been trying. We need to go in a different direction."

"I couldn't agree with you more. That's why we are here talking right now. Here's what I'm proposing. You enter our medical school. What you don't know, we'll let you catch up on. The cost for your medical training will be free, and we'll still pay you your same salary. Then we will move you into a house with four bedrooms. The hospital owns a four-bedroom house a stone's throw from the hospital parking lot.

"Albert will move there as well. We will have a nurse or a medical tech in one of the guest rooms during the day. After that, you would need to buzz us if something was wrong. Albert's bored and depressed, so I recommend some changes for him. I think we can give him a mobile chair/ bed. He could move it around in the house.

"We are going to change his treatment again. It's time to try stem cell injections. We've known they can work. We were trying some things that we didn't know whether they would work. So we tried some of them. We've noticed no physical changes. In other words, Albert's spinal cord still has a short circuit. The impulses are not passing through the cut. So we are going to inject some stem cells into that junction and see if some connections will regenerate.

"Allie, something else on your part. I want you to be more sensual with Albert."

Allie's face was one of disgust. "You are out of your mind. He can't have sex."

Smiling, Cheryl stated the obvious. "You're not a man, darling. A man's mind works differently from yours. Men are very visual. What they see can stimulate them. I want you to stimulate Albert. You are a very beautiful lady. I want him to see you up close. I want you to get on the bed with him, kiss his cheek, run your hands through his hair. When it's time, kiss him on the lips. Encourage him to recover."

"What comes to mind is a whore."

"Sex is not evil. We are trying some different things. I know you have an attachment to him. It's more than wanting a patient to get better. Albert is not getting better. He's the same as he was nine months ago. He is not trying anymore. His will to live is dying. We need to wake it back up while we still can. We need him to try. Allie, you can be the change factor."

"Okay, so logic didn't work. Now you're laying a guilt trip on me."

"Honey, the truth is you are the magic in his life. Without you, he would have died nine months ago out there in that field. Without you,

Albert would have died in the ER. When everyone else gave up, you didn't. I watched as the others gave up. You pounded on his chest. You fought for him. Why? Are you done doing everything possible to help him now? I'm sorry. We're finished here then." She turned and gave her back to Allie.

Allie stood there for a moment. "You don't hold back much."

Dr. Hastings swung around again. "Where is that Allie that pounded on Albert's chest? That's the Allie I need right now," she said as she pounded on her desk and then turned and faced the window.

"Okay, I'll be your whore. Shouldn't I change my name to Star or Easy?"

Some modifications had to be made to the house for Albert's new wheelchair to be able to get to his bedroom, kitchen, and living room. The hospital bought all the groceries for the house, except for any alcoholic beverages. Even the fridge could be opened by Albert's computer. A door was added to the wall separating Albert's and Allie's bedrooms.

Then the hospital paid movers to move Allie in. After she got settled, Albert was moved in with all his equipment. The third bedroom held more equipment to receive signals from some of the portable devices that Albert carried on his wheelchair (mobile hospital bed).

Allie briefed Albert on the new strategy. He would start injections of stem cells. Afterward, she began his physical therapy. Albert normally wore shorts and a T-shirt. He had a catheter for the urine and a diaperlike pad for the other. Today Allie was wearing shorts and a tank top only. For the first time ever, she hopped up onto his chair/bed and began massaging his feet.

Albert was still just in his black box. Two fingers were working. His face muscles were not working, but inside, he was smiling. Allie looked great. He thought she didn't need all those other clothes. Shorts and a tank top were plenty. He could even go for less. Inside his box, he was shaking his head no, but nothing was really moving.

Then Allie started working on his calves and then his thighs. Albert was aware of the change, and he liked it—a lot. Her gym shorts were as revealing as her tank top.

Allie moved to his chest and shoulders. As she worked, she moved down close to his face. Albert looked at the body of Allie and was in awe at how beautiful she was. She seemed perfect. He was seeing more and more skin. She was close enough for him to smell her, and he liked that.

Now she sat on him as if he were a horse. This allowed her to rub both shoulders at the same time. As she rubbed, she started rocking back and forth. She was surprised at how good this felt to her as well.

Albert had no feelings on anything she touched, but he wished he could. He watched as little beads of sweat built on her body. His eyes moved from her breast to her eyes and back to her breast. When he thought it couldn't get any better, she bent down and kissed his cheek. This allowed a closer look at her chest—braless. There were beads of sweat forming there as well. Allie was still rocking back and forth. She enjoyed his response and found that she liked what she was doing.

Allie leaned over Albert a little lower again and stroked his hair. She dragged her fingernails down his cheek and then through his hair. Again, he could feel nothing except dream of what it felt like. She took both hands and touched his cheeks, pushing her hands together. She reached down, pushing her body down hard onto his, and kissed him. She kissed his forehead as well. Her breast were close enough for Albert to smell. He couldn't feel any of the touching, but his sense of smell was working just fine.

Allie kept rocking the whole time. Her senses were all working, and she liked the feeling. And then she came. Allie actually had an orgasm, and she let Albert know. "Oh my goodness, I didn't expect that."

Dr. Hastings had been right. Albert needed some affection, but so did Allie. After a short time, she got off Albert and just lay next to him on the bed/chair. She continued to play with his hair.

While she was snuggling with him, Albert wrote onto his tablet, "Allie, what was that?"

"They call it having sex."

Again, writing on the tablet with two fingers was slow. "Don't tease me. Why do that?"

"Albert, we just moved in together. It's quite normal to have sex with the guy you are sharing a home with."

"Get up. Go away until tell truth."

Allie got up on her elbow, and then looking into Albert's eyes, she replied, "The truth is that I made a friend on a plane. He tried to die out in a field. After that, the ER doc wanted to unplug you. I screamed at my new friend and pounded on his chest as they dragged me away. I screamed one more time, and you moved your finger, and the sensor beeped. Then it beeped again and again. Now here we are.

"Dr. Hastings said we needed to try some different things. She suggested sex. I thought she was crazy, but I agreed to touch you more."

Albert was smiling on the inside. "I liked it."

"Me too, Albert." Allie lay back down with a big smile on her face. "Me too."

The feelings he had were that he was in a closet. He could stick his two fingers out. He could see and smell what was outside the closet, but there were no physical feelings. Albert did have memories of him and Liz doing similar things. He had feelings then, and it was great.

Chapter 10

OCTOBER 15, 2031

During the next few weeks, some amazing things started happening with Albert. The God-given magic in the stem cells produced some dramatic changes in Albert's ability to reconnect electronically with his body. Albert's nerve impulses, stimuli, started reconnecting with the sensory receptors.

One morning as Allie woke up at her usual time, something felt different. She had her arm wrapped around Albert, but he was holding her hand. "Albert, do you notice anything different?"

Inside his box, he shook his head.

"Do you feel this?" Then she wiggled her hand. "You were holding my hand?"

With that, he let go and raised his arm to look at his left hand. Then he typed. "What going on?"

"I guess some things are getting reconnected."

Without thinking, he turned his head. He pushed with his right arm and found that it too was working. Nothing happened when he tried to use his right hand. This was just the beginning.

Albert started doing more of the things that his body normally did automatically. His eyelids started working. Now he didn't need as many man-made devices. The reconnection continued. Easily, half the thirteen million neurons had now reconnected. He could breathe on his own. Parts of the cervical nerves, including the brachial plexus, started getting some action. Now all of Albert's fingers on his left hand were working. There was no real grip yet. He could raise both arms, but his right hand was not functioning. His arms were weak; it had been a year since he had used them. His hearing had been working, but now it was better.

With the lumbar, there were no signals moving to the brain, possibly being blocked by a scar tissue. That meant that his legs were not working. However, his sacral nerves were passing impulses normally. That meant his bowels and bladder continued working. His crotch area was now alive and well.

Dr. Hastings was concerned about the stop in the reception and the transfer of impulses to the brain. A scar tissue must have formed over part of the spinal cord connection. So they now included some placenta with the stem cell injections. Dr. Hastings was willing to try anything to help Albert reconnect as much as possible.

Allie continued her physical therapy. Of course, she noticed Albert's chest being more active. She began to lightly drag her nails over his skin surface. One day when she bent to kiss him, he puckered his lips on his own. More of his body was waking up.

Albert had some activities he needed to do on his own. He was given a pair of small weights for his hands as he started moving his arms. The right hand was not working, but Velcro made up for that. They also attached a brace like a gymnast might use on the parallel bars. With this device, his right hand could help his left hand on the tablet.

Something new in Allie's life was medical school. She had classroom assignments and also hospital and clinical time working with patients. Her clinical time for now was with her one patient, Albert. Anne worked with her as she practiced giving shots, taking blood pressure readings, and installing and removing catheters. At the house, an RN continued to monitor her basic skills.

Her physical therapy on Albert usually came at the end of her day. Then she would snuggle with her patient, sometimes falling asleep. Both liked sleeping together. Even going to the next room to sleep was no longer pleasing to either. Allie and Albert were developing a deep relationship.

Albert had lost 25 percent of his body weight after one year. He went from 195 to 150 pounds. He looked too thin. His body fat had gone away, and now he was beginning to lose muscle. His throat was better now. He could drink his Ensure and even small pieces of food like peas and rice. Albert needed to pick up another 10 or 15 pounds.

Allie and Albert found they could have real sex if she only removed the tip of the catheter. Allie's medical skills had some personal benefits. Albert's attitude had done just what Dr. Hastings had hoped. He was alive and working at becoming more self-sufficient. One evening as she was kissing Albert, she found that his tongue was getting some feeling back.

BOOK IV

REHAB

Chapter 11

APRIL 10, 2032

A llie woke up for the fourth morning in a row not feeling well. She thought she might be coming down with the flu. Anne told her she might have a different kind of sickness. They tested her, and she was, in fact, pregnant with Albert's child.

Allie told Albert she was carrying his fourth child. "Okay, Albert, I need a full-time man in my life now. I'm pregnant with your fourth child."

Albert was elated and sad at the same time. On his tablet, he wrote, "I love you, Allie. Wish stand. Improved much, wish stand beside you, say I do." Albert's mind was normal, but he wrote in a kind of shorthand. Anne came in on their private meeting driving Albert's new electric wheelchair. "Albert, I think I can help you out here in the short term and the long term.\ We have leg braces that you can wear now. With the help of a walker, you can stand and lock your legs. You can stand next to your bride. I wouldn't walk very far this way, but you can move around a little bit."

"Okay. Long term?"

"There is a possibility that we can tap into your brain and talk with your legs to have them move just as if you told them to. That would involve a little more surgery. Let's wait on that just in case your legs decide to start working."

"Okay, take braces now."

"I might as well tell you that there is something new coming. The VW people want to give us a hybrid minivan. It will be driven on autopilot. You push a button, and a platform comes out for your wheelchair. Then you drive up to the front, and on your tablet, punch in where you want to go. It will have twenty-five preset locations, and then you can also type in a specific one."

"Anne. Need see family."

Chapter 12

APRIL 24, 2032

Liz had left a corpse on a table those fifteen months ago, and now she and the kids were meeting that corpse for lunch. Life had gone on as normal after she left the hospital that day. She felt guilty, but she had taken the money and the divorce from the hospital. Now Albert had come back from the brink of death and wanted to meet with the family.

A deep sadness swallowed Liz. She wondered about leaving her husband. She had continued seeing Richard. He had been a friend, and then he became a very good friend. Meanwhile, her husband and the father of her three kids lay in a coma in the VA hospital.

Anne met the Mendoza family at the Burger King near Highway 55 and Forty-Sixth Street. Liz had brought the kids. Now they waited for a VW van to show up. Albert had twenty-five settings for locations to drive to but had only used a few so far. The newest setting was the address of the Burger King. The red-and-white van pulled in and parked in the handicap slot. The van door slid open. A ramp moved to its place, and an electric chair drove out and into the lot.

Albert had grown his hair back, so you couldn't see the scalp scars. But the cheek scars were there. Also, he had lost fifty pounds. But he was Dad, Albert.

Anne told them, "He can communicate with you, but he does not have a voice yet. He can talk using his tablet. Just be patient."

The first thing they all did was run up and hug Dad. Liz felt bad for not visiting him. She hung back until he waved her up. Then they hugged, and both cried. The children couldn't believe their father was alive. He was much thinner but alive. Jessica didn't want to let go.

Anne stepped in and directed traffic. "Let's get some Whopper meals on me." So they all moved inside and ordered. Albert typed his order, and his tablet spoke. The teens were impressed.

After they all sat down, Albert hit a button on his tablet, and it started to speak. "For now, this is my voice. I've typed this ahead of time to speed things up. I'm sure Mom told you what happened to me, but let me tell you from my point of view. I had just put my briefcase in the overhead bin and taken my seat. Allie was a steward directing traffic near my seat, an exit row. We spoke briefly after my flight was cancelled. I told her that I would have to drive my Jeep to Denver. I took off heading down Highway 77. I was going to pick up I-35 and head south down to I-80. On Highway 77, six cars crashed after running onto some black ice. A window came out and cut the top of my head off. Of course, I don't remember it, but I was told that's what happened.

"Meanwhile, the steward returned home and had a big fight with her boyfriend. She ran out of the house and started driving. She wound up on 77 and the accident. My Jeep was there with no top. For some reason, she stopped to see if it was, in fact, my Jeep. By now, my body was frozen. Allie found me, and I was missing something. The top of the Jeep was on another twenty feet. She walked toward it and found my frozen top. I'm told she was in a state of shock at this point. She picked it up and was coming back toward me. Dr. Anne here saw her and took my top and put it back on.

"Anne told me Allie looked like a zombie. Anne tried to get her to go home, but she wouldn't leave until they came to get me. They covered me up again, and Allie got a blanket as well. After she calmed down, she started talking. As she spoke, she decided to tell me she was tired of this world and would take enough sleeping pills to leave it. By this time, I was thawing out. I could hear everything going on, including Allie. I felt like I was in a black box. I couldn't move anything. When she mentioned killing herself, I screamed no as loud as I could.

"No sound came out of me, but my middle finger moved. Allie screamed and hopped up. Dr. Anne saw her and asked what was going on. She told her I was alive. For me, this was the first time I knew that they didn't know that I was alive. Dr. Anne told Allie that it was quite normal for dead people to twitch. I thought, 'Hello, I'm not dead.' Dr. Anne got Allie calmed down, and Allie sat back down.

"Allie told me that I was dead and she would be joining me later that night. Again I screamed no. Again, Allie screamed and jumped up, mumbling, 'He's alive. Albert's alive.'

"Again, Dr. Anne came over. Allie explained that I had twitched again. Dr. Anne said, 'He's got to do it for me.' The short version is I did.

"They took us to the ER. They did a lot of work on a corpse, and then I was told by Allie I had to twitch again. I screamed again, but nothing happened. The ER doctor told them to unplug me. Allie screamed at me again, 'No, Albert! If you die tonight, so do I!' Then she pounded on my chest several times before they dragged her away.

"Her pounding had broken free my neuron to allow my finger to move. They had already taken out my breathing tube. I screamed again, my finger moved, and the sensor beeped. Everything grew quiet, so I did it again. Then people started clapping. I'm told Allie was clapping and jumping around. Something had finally gone right. Dr. Anne got my breathing tube replaced quickly. At least I was alive for the moment. They induced a medical coma so that my top could heal without me moving around.

"Your mom released me to the hospital for research. I'm alive today because of that. But for about a year, I lived inside a box. I mean, we found that I had two fingers on my left hand that worked. Also, I had my vision, but my eyelids weren't on the same page. They got my eyelids working with little machines. They could be controlled by my tablet.

"Toward the end of 2031, they moved me and the steward, Allie, to a house belonging to the hospital. Early on, Dr. Hastings had hired Allie away from the airlines. After we settled into our new home, the doctors began injecting a formula involving stem cells into the place my spinal cord had been severed. This chemical compound started growing new connections with the spinal cord. Right now, they are saying that about half my neurons have reconnected.

"I was being kept alive by machines. In the last few weeks, they began taking away the different machines. I've been on a feeding tube for a year. It will stay in for a while. My throat has started working a little bit, so I can swallow this shake, rice, and other things I don't need to chew. Now I wake up to coffee in the mornings. The hospital staff takes care of me during the day, and Allie has the night shift.

"Before you get to ask me questions, I need to know what's been happening in your world."

James was eighteen at five ten. He was a senior, graduating on the first week of June. Mike was sixteen at five eleven. He was a sophomore. Jessica was fifteen at five foot five. She was a freshman. Liz was the same size as her daughter. Except for a few wrinkles, they would look like twins.

"Jessica."

"I'm a freshman. I played volleyball this year. I started on the freshman squad. I like several boys, and none of them are freshmen. I'm doing the college prep route. My grades are good. I'm active in the church youth group. We do pizza night and weekend retreats, and we did a Super Bowl party.

"Mike."

"I'm an inch taller than James. And I'm doing football. You have to do PE, so I'm doing football. Don't know about next year. I'm a tight end. School is going okay. I'm not doing the honors thing. I'm thinking

I'll get out of school and make some money, do some traveling. You've done a lot of traveling."

Albert didn't have a comment. He nodded to James.

"For me, school is fun. I've got everything set to graduate in June, one more month of classes. I've got a date for the prom. Life is good, Dad."

"Okay, don't have to make up a year and a half this afternoon. But I need to tell you a little more. I've typed. Just listen."

Albert clicked on the other recorded message. "This will be a little hard to listen to, but stay with me until the end. December 14, 2030, I died. The top of my head was separated from my body, decapitated. Because I had made a new friend on the plane, Allie, I would live. I was locked inside my body. Everyone, including Allie, thought me dead. But I wasn't quite. My hearing and vision were working. My middle finger moved if I screamed. From that night to here, Allie has kept me alive. After almost a year, I had given up. Nothing had worked like they had hoped.

"Dr. Hastings was ready to try some different things. They moved me into a house with Allie. For that year, she had been my only friend. The hospital was paying her a salary to be a medical technician. She did physical therapy on me. I still could only feel my two fingers. They were outside the box, but everything else was still inside. I had given up.

"So I was moved into a house with Allie on the hospital grounds. She continued my treatment. She made me feel as good as possible. They started using a formula that included stem cells, God's little building blocks. Gradually, my body started reconnecting. I'm referring to my neurons. It truly made a miracle happen.

"I was locked in a coffin with only two fingers sticking out. Now I'm out of the box. I don't have a voice yet. My face is showing some life, including my tongue. The neurons might be done reconnecting. We don't know yet. This is where we are at today. You saw me pull up in a new van. The experiment continues. Are you ready for one more thing for today?"

Albert locked his legs and stood up using his crutches. Each of the kids came by and hugged Albert. Then he waved for Liz.

Albert had anticipated Liz's feeling guilty. He punched one more prerecorded message. "Don't feel any guilt about my life. The doctors told you to go on with your life. You were a good wife, and you've been a great mom. I was a corpse. You allowed the hospital to open that coffin. Now I'm standing up, with some help. I'm talking with you. This tablet is my voice for today."

Liz was crying again. She felt she shouldn't have given up. And she had gone on with her life.

Albert punched another pretyped message on his tablet. "Kids, we need to get together again soon. It doesn't require all three together at the same time. I've got a house on the VA hospital parking lot. Look for a red-and-white van."

Jessica asked, "What about our questions?"

"Next time."

They all exchanged phone numbers and e-mail addresses. Then they watched as Albert mounted his steed, the van, and drove off.

Chapter 13

JUNE 4, 2032

Time passed rapidly for Albert. He was now able to make some sounds, but he always kept the tablet close. Allie was working twelve-hour days six days a week and inching forward in her medical studies.

Now it was graduation day for James at Roosevelt High School. This year, 248 seniors would walk across the stage. It looked like clear skies for the ceremony out on the football field. There was a section for wheelchairs up front, and Albert and Allie took advantage of it.

The school had done an amazing job with the planning. Everything worked. Graduation is an exciting time that can't be over quickly enough. The parents wanted to watch their student get his or her diploma but not all 248. The speakers knew they needed to speak briefly because the parents came to watch their student get his or her diploma. Afterward, it was time to go and celebrate. The juniors were cheering because they were now the top dogs on campus. Freshmen are cheering because they were no longer freshmen.

The graduates have completed their childhood, but it doesn't make them adults. They have everything they need to become an adult, but now they have to step into the shoes of responsibility. There are several options out there, but none will be easy. James had chosen to train to become a mason. Albert knew his father, Alberto, would have been very proud.

The guys brought their special friends, but Jessica hadn't settled on just one. Liz and Richard would meet them at the Olive Garden on I-494. Today was a special day for James and the first time the family met Allie. The Italian food was terrific. The kids had known Richard for a while. The small talk was enjoyed, and then it was time to leave.

Albert agreed to drop off his kids at their mom's place. The VW van was loaded up, and they took off. Jessica asked, "Now, Dad?"

The van was on autopilot, heading to his old house. Albert was willing to answer some questions. "Sure. But I will give short answers." Albert was still relying on his voice on the tablet.

Jessica asked, "How did you keep going with no improvement for a year?"

"Like living in box. Memories, you guys, Liz, my new friend, Allie. Some staff spoke to me like machine. Allie spoke to me like I was a real person, a real friend. Got depressed, frustrated living in box. I see and hear Allie. Life better. Moved to house, great. See more Allie. Life better. Survived because of Allie. Now we get married."

That was a big surprise for the kids. Mike spoke first. "Holy cow, Dad. Aren't you moving kind of fast here?'"

"Actually, moving slow. She's going to have my fourth child in six months."

Again, the teens were shocked. Now the van grew silent. Albert didn't push the moment. It would take a little time for his family to absorb the news. As they opened the van door, more hugs and kisses were exchanged. James spoke up. "That was a lot of news today, Dad. Know that we love you and want to be around you a lot."

As Albert moved up in the company, he spent more time away from his family. Now he had time for them, and he would enjoy it. "Okay, James. Where train?"

"That's a good question. Why not with you, Dad?"

The wave goodbye didn't pass on the surprise of the idea. Albert thought he could do that.

Chapter 14

JUNE 12, 2032

Today's wedding in the hospital chapel was a total secret, so Anne had to work hard to find out anything. Allie had asked for ten days of leave beginning today. So that meant the wedding would be today. Alice, the retired volunteer at the information desk, had kept a watch out for Allie. When Allie walked in with a handsome young man, Alice started her notification process. Anne was called and told the situation. Anne notified her people to include James.

Chaplain Scott had an office next to the chapel, so his movement wasn't noticed. Albert came in the back way unnoticed and went straight to the chapel. Allie and her elder brother walked in the front door like nothing special was happening, carrying a big clothing bag. Dr. Hastings used the service elevator to hide her movement. Now all the wedding party was in place. Chaplain Scott played the wedding song, and Eric escorted his sister down the aisle. Allie was now in all white and stood next to her Albert.

Chaplain Scott spoke. "I think everyone who was invited is here. Shall we begin?"

Everyone looked at the chaplain like, *Let's go.*

Chaplain Scott began with a prayer. "Heavenly Father, we give you thanks for today and for this ceremony. We commit everything to you. In Jesus's name, we offer this prayer. Amen."

As if right on cue, the chapel door was opened by Nurse Johnston. She said, "Don't mind us. We're just coming in for our midafternoon prayer. Just continue with what you're doing."

Thirty staff members filed in and took their seats. Last to file in were James, Mike, and Jessica. All three had big smiles. They came and sat in the front.

Allie asked, "Are you here for the midafternoon prayer as well?"

Mike asked, "Why? Did we miss it?"

Chaplain Scott looked at Anne and asked, "Are we waiting on anyone else?"

Anne replied, "Go on with whatever you were doing. We just came to pray."

Chaplain Scott went on to talk about marriage and the fact that it was a holy union between two. "Let these rings symbolize your promises to each other. Albert Mendoza, do you take Allie Blain to be your wife?"

Albert stood for the ceremony looking into Allie's eyes. He said, "I do." Albert didn't actually speak much, but he made himself understood. Chaplain Scott asked Allie the same question. "Allie Blain, do you take Albert Mendoza to be your husband?"

Allie agreed. "I do."

Cheryl couldn't believe she just witnessed Albert's total transformation. Nineteen months ago, he was a corpse, and now he was getting married to his pregnant fiancée.

Chaplain Scott pronounced, "Because of the commitments you've made today, you are now legally husband and wife, Albert Mendoza and Allie Blain. Albert, you may kiss the bride." And he did.

Allie had chosen to keep her last name in honor of the neighbor who said, "I am my brother's keeper." The baby would be a Mendoza.

Jumping up to congratulate their father and Allie were the three teens. Then the rest of the prayer group offered their congratulations as well. At this point, a cake was brought in with some coffee and punch.

Albert and Allie left for a week in Houston. Eric welcomed them to his huge home. In 2016, he bought it for $600,000. Now it was worth $2 million. Eric rented a van with a lift for the week. There were too many people for Albert to remember all the names, except Chandler, her other brother. Mostly, they stayed around Eric's home. There was an overnight trip to San Antonio. There, the shoe was on the other foot. Allie met too many people from Albert's family to remember all their names.

Chapter 15

JUNE 22, 2032

Both Albert and Allie were content and exhausted. They needed a few days to recover from their fun-filled honeymoon. There's no place like home and your own bed. The two couldn't remember a time when they were happier or more content.

James's remark about training with his father was still in the forefront of Albert's mind. The first person he would need to meet with would be Cheryl. The second would be his old boss at Baseline Brick, Javier Cantu.

Albert scheduled some time with Cheryl. He told her he would go there. Enough of Albert had reconnected to make him feel very independent. He drove across the parking lot and up to the neurology department. "Good morning, Doctor. I'm ready for some more experimenting. I would like your help in getting a visit with the dean of instruction at Minneapolis Community and Technical College. I would like to teach there part time. You could tell them my story and that you want to continue testing my recovery." Albert was able to speak, but it was not crisp and clear. He spoke slowly.

"Thank you for imagining new ideas for me. So you are interested in teaching students to become masons? Dr. Pierce is a friend of mine. He will at least talk with you. I'll set that up."

Then Albert made an appointment with Javier Cantu, the CEO of Baseline Brick. Albert showed up for his appointment on his new wheelchair. Albert greeted Mr. Cantu's secretary. "Hello, Donna. I have a three o'clock meeting with Mr. Cantu." These simple sentences were spread out and said with great determination.

"He has a meeting with an Albert Blain. Guess you tried to fool us?"

"Actually, I just wanted to speak with Javier without a lot of fanfare. If I had used my name, then a lot of people might have shown up, and I wouldn't really be able to visit with Javier."

"You're right. We were very worried about you. I'll buzz him and have him come out here." She buzzed Javier, and then she came around the desk to hug her longtime friend.

"*Hijole*, Albert. You're Albert Blain also? Last I heard, you were in a coma."

"Hello, my friend. I was in a car accident. Had my spinal cord snap. This is where I'm at today." Then Albert stood up.

"I'm amazed, Albert. It is so good to see you. How's the family?"

"Liz released me to the hospital so they could experiment with me. They told her to go on with her life. I was a corpse basically. She released me, and the hospital got her a divorce. Since, I've married the lady who saved my life, and we are expecting a child. James graduated earlier this month and said he wanted to be a mason. He asked me to be involved with his training. I've got a meeting over at MCTC next week. I wanted you to see me and know that I'm interested in teaching my son and others how to lay brick." When Albert spoke, it was not like a normal conversation. He had to really focus on his pronunciation. Albert was learning to speak all over again.

"You certainly were our best mason."

"That's what I need you to tell him. I have a handicap, but I'm sure we can find a way around that." Albert needed to know how Javier's family was doing, and after that, he mounted his autopilot van again for the VA hospital parking lot.

After a few days of rest, Allie started back in on her medical training, six days a week with twelve-hour days. Her clinical time now involved a lot more than Albert. She was careful not to attempt to do too much. At the end of one more week, it was obvious that she needed to take a leave from her medical studies, and so she took off the rest of the year.

Chapter 16

JULY 1, 2032

Albert took his van over to Minneapolis Community and Technical College (MCTC) at 1501 Hennepin Avenue. It was close to the intersection of I-94 and I-394. MCTC was a school that was growing and figuring out how to better prepare young people for jobs in and around the Twin Cities. There was some new construction on campus, and that meant that it was still expanding.

Albert directed the van to park in a van-accessible handicap parking space. Then he exited the van and headed toward the administration building. Dr. Pierce was easy to find. His office was on the first floor. Albert was shown right in. "Good afternoon, Mr. Mendoza, and welcome to Minneapolis Community and Technical College. I understand you've gone through quite a lot over the last two years."

Every day found Albert speaking better. There were smaller breaks between words. "Dr. Pierce, it's good to meet you. That's kind of what I'm here to talk with you about. My spinal cord was cut free from my brain. For a year, I lived in a box with only two of my fingers sticking out. My sight worked, but I couldn't move anything else. We began trying stem cells. Now I'm about half reconnected. My son just graduated from high school and wants to be a mason. I know you don't have a mason program. I'm here to see if we can start some training for masons. I remember my days at the junior college in San Antonio. I went through training to work as a mason but also had some academic work. It was beneficial later on in my career. Mr. Javier Cantu of Baseline Brick started sending me out to put in bids for his company on different projects. You can call him if you'd like to verify what I am saying."

"Dr. Hastings gave me his name, and we have already spoken. I'm afraid it's too late to set up anything for this fall semester, but we can look into it in the future."

"Javier called me and told me that he had nine people ready to commit to the training. With my son, that makes ten. They can do academics on the MWF schedule. TTh, the students can put in three hours of fieldwork. That fieldwork can easily be set up. It would be laying free brick for someone. It could be on MCTC or one of Mr. Cantu's buildings. Those details can be decided later."

"Mr. Mendoza, how much salary would you require?"

"My first year would be free. If you like the program, then we can talk about paying me."

"Mr. Mendoza, I think we can say you have a deal. Bring your students in three weeks." The impossible had just happened. A new program was just set in place without costing the school any dollars. Dr. Pierce was smiling as big as his face would allow.

Then the academic dean, Dr. Sharon Peel, was brought in to the meeting, and she liked the concept. Dr. Peel referred Albert to Professor Young, in charge of program development. "Good morning, Dr. Young."

"Call me Neil. Dr. Pierce said you were coming by with a new plan."

"Yes and no. I want to enroll ten students into the new mason apprentice program."

"Albert, we don't have a mason apprentice program."

"That's part of the yes and no. I have the plan, and I'm told you can put it into ink." Really, it wasn't a problem. They used a skeleton plan from a different program and just changed the name.

ASSOCIATE OF ARTS
MASONRY
Apprentice Program

I.   Communication – 9 hours (* required subject)

    A. English 101*
    B. English 102*
    C. Speech 101*

II.   Social/Behavioral Sciences – 9 hours required

Examples include but not limited to

    A. Anthropology
    B. Economics
    C. Geography
    D. Cultural Economics
    E. World History Part I
    F. U.S. History through 1865
    G. U.S. History after 1865

III.   Life/Physical Sciences – 9 hours required

Examples include but not limited to

    A. 101 Biology
    B. 102 Biology
    C. 105 Microbes
    D. 106 Animals
    E. 107 Botany
    F. 112 Humans
    G. 144 DNA/ Heredity

H. Ecology

I. 101 Astronomy

J. 101 Chemistry

K. 111 Weather

L. 112 Landforms

M. 129 Life in Our Universe

N. 101 Physics

O. 224 Senses

P. 201 Engineering

IV. Humanities/Arts – 9 hours required

Examples include but not limited to

A. 101 American Literature

B. 102 American Literature

C. 103 English Literature

D. 104 English Literature

E. 101 Introduction to Spanish

F. 101 Introduction to German

G. 101 Introduction to Russian

H. 236 Comparative Religions

I. 250 History of Civilization

J. 255 Philosophy

K. 260 Ethics

L. 101 Art

M. 208 Renaissance and Baroque Art

N. 210 Modern Art

O. 101 Music

P. 101 Introduction to Theater

V.   Mathematics – 3 hours required

Examples include but not limited to

    A. 101 General
    B. 102 Structures
    C. 101 Algebra
    D. 201 Mathematics for Business

VI.   Computer Sciences – 3 hours required

Examples include but not limited to

    A. 101 Introduction to Computers
    B. 102 Intermediate Course in Computers
    C. 103 Advanced Course in Computers
    D. 104 Programming

VII. Fieldwork – 15 hours of credit

    (for the 4 semesters)
    Location TBD

VIII. Electives – 6 hours

TOTAL – 63 hours of credit to receive THE DEGREE OF ASSOCIATE OF ARTS IN MASONRY

    This is a two-year program that can be continued into a four-year-degree path. All academics will take place on campus in the MWF schedule. All fieldwork will be accomplished during the TTh schedule. Usually, our courses are three-hour classes. It will total 63 hours of credit in all. If you choose to continue onto a four-year program, all of these hours will count toward that degree.

Chapter 17

JULY 22, 2032

Albert was introduced to eleven guy applicants and four lady applicants. Dr. Young was surprised at the number. He was expecting only nine or ten. "Ladies and gentlemen, welcome. This is the first time we have offered this course. Mr. Mendoza is a master mason. A car accident on Highway 77 has moved him into the classroom instead of working outside on buildings. He knows everything about masonry. On the night of his car accident, he was on his way to Denver to bid on a project that involved several million dollars. I'm sorry about his accident, but I'm grateful that he is now here at MCTC sharing what he has learned. He has produced several award-winning buildings, so trust him, and you will finish this program. Enjoy the ride."

Albert had his son James pass out the folders that had in them what the new recruits would need. For the nine, their companies were paying for their training. James's tuition was reduced because his father worked for MCTC. Others might need some tuition assistance. Those forms were also in the packet.

"When you leave today, we should have your projected schedule for four semesters. If you decide later that you want to switch a class, we can do that. On Monday, August 23, I will give you your schedule for the first semester. It will show class times and locations. At that time, you should buy your books for the semester. Most classes require one book, but some will have workbooks. On August 23, I will give you more information.

"In four semesters, you will become masonry apprentices with an associate of arts degree. Graduation is scheduled for May 5, 2034. Classes begin September 13 and run through December 6. They will pick up again on January 24 and run through May 6. You will have the summer free. Classes will start again on September 12 and run through December 9. Your last semester will begin on January 23 and run through May 3, with graduation on the fifth.

"Let me talk with you about your clothes. What you wear to school will represent all of us. If you want to rebel, do it at the club but not here at school. Come dressed sharp. On fieldwork days, we have a dress code as well. Don't show any skin. That means long pants and long sleeves. Ladies, I recommend a ponytail. Bib overalls are fine. Come wearing boots. You will not look great, but you will be glad you are covered. Don't wear anything that you like a lot. It will get messy. One more thing, nobody carries anything for anybody. You wanted to do this, so then you will carry your own stuff. If that bothers you, then get a different job."

After the orientation, Albert was amazed with everything. He was going to have a lot of time with his son, and he could still be useful. He had been released from his box. He didn't need his legs because he was flying high. Albert and James ate at the Chili's on campus. He and James were reconnecting like his neurons.

Albert didn't know it, but some opposition to his program had risen. Drs. Pierce and Peel were placed on probation for not following school procedures. The real problem was that Dr. Pierce had enemies on the faculty. This was a little ammunition for those opposing him. The school board liked the idea of the program, but Drs. Pierce and

Peel must follow the rules. The plan would go ahead for this year, but now it would go through the proper channels.

To her secretary, Dr. Peel said, "Two things. First, find out who fussed. Second, find out some dirt on whomever fussed. I'll need some ammunition to shut them up."

Holly answered, "You got it, Doc."

www.ingramcontent.com/pod-product-compliance
Lightning Source LLC
Chambersburg PA
CBHW050500110726
47899CB00003B/1020